HELLO KITTY®

A Day of Thanks

Abrams Books for Young Readers
New York

One beautiful day, Hello Kitty's teacher asks his students to write an essay about what they are most thankful for.

When Hello Kitty gets home after school, she thinks about what she should write. What would be a good subject for her essay?

Hello Kitty is thankful for all her books. She loves when Mama reads to her before she goes to sleep.

Hello Kitty is thankful for her tricycle. She loves when she goes with Papa for rides around the neighborhood.

Hello Kitty is thankful for apple pie. She loves helping Grandma bake in the kitchen.

Hello Kitty is thankful for her new paint set. She loves painting pictures with Grandpa.

Hello Kitty is thankful for her tutu. She loves to dance with Mimmy.

Hello Kitty is thankful for her camera.

She loves to take pictures with her friend Dear Daniel.

Hello Kitty is thankful for school, where she learns new things with her friends.

Hello Kitty still isn't sure what she should write her essay about.

THANKSGIVING

Suddenly, she realizes what she is most thankful for.

Hello Kitty is most thankful for all her wonderful friends and family! They make every day special.

Library of Congress Cataloging-in-Publication Data
Hello Kitty a day of thanks / by Sanrio
pages cm
ISBN 978-1-4197-1842-7 (paperback)
I. Sanrio, Kabushiki Kaisha.
PZ7.1.H447 2015
[E]—dc23
2015000345

Book design by Alissa Faden

Printed and bound in China
10 9 8 7 6 5 4 3 2 1

Abrams Books for Young Readers are available at special discounts when
purchased in quantity for premiums and promotions as well as fundraising
or educational use. Special editions can also be created to specification. For
details, contact specialsales@abramsbooks.com or the address below.

115 West 18th Street
New York, NY 10011
www.abramsbooks.com